For Dakotah, Luke, Skylar, and Sophia—four kids with great skulls
—B. T.

For Sally's skull, and everything in and around it
—S. C.

ATHENEUM BOOKS FOR YOUNG READERS

An imprint of Simon & Schuster Children's Publishing Division

1230 Avenue of the Americas, New York, New York 10020

Text copyright © 2019 by Blair Thornburgh

Illustrations copyright © 2019 by Scott Campbell

For information about special discounts for bulk purchases,

please contact Simon & Schuster Special Sales at 1-866-506-1949 or business@simonandschuster.com.

The Simon & Schuster Speakers Bureau can bring authors to your live event. For more information or to book an event,

contact the Simon & Schuster Speakers Bureau at 1-866-248-3049 or visit our website at www.simonspeakers.com.

Book design by Sonia Chaghatzbanian

The text for this book was set in Garden Pro.

The illustrations for this book were rendered in watercolor.

Manufactured in China

0519 SCP

First Edition

2 4 6 8 10 9 7 5 3 1

Library of Congress Cataloging-in-Publication Data

Names: Thornburgh, Blair, author. | Campbell, Scott, 1973– illustrator.

Title: Skulls! / Blair Thornburgh ; illustrated by Scott Campbell.

Description: First edition. | New York : Atheneum Books for Young Readers, [2019] | Audience: Ages 4–8. | Audience: K to grade 3.

Identifiers: LCCN 2017045045 | ISBN 9781534414006 (hardcover) | ISBN 9781534414013 (eBook)

Subjects: LCSH: Skull–Juvenile literature. | Human skeleton–Juvenile literature. | Bones–Juvenile literature.

Classification: LCC QL822 .T46 2019 | DDC 612.7/51–dc23

LC record available at https://lccn.loc.gov/2017045045

SKULLS!

Blair Thornburgh

Illustrated by Scott Campbell

A Atheneum Books for Young Readers • New York London Toronto Sydney New Delhi
atheneum

You probably don't think much about skulls.

But every head
of every person
you've ever seen . . .

has a skull inside.
This is a good thing.

Skulls take a while to grow strong and hard,
but it's time well spent.

Skulls are safe and snug,
like a car seat for your brain.

Skulls give your face a good shape.

Skulls let your jaws snap.

Skulls hold your teeth in place . . .

until they don't.

Skulls have holes in them . . .

Hole

Hole

Hole

Hole

Hole

Hole

Hole

for sounds,

for light,

for air,

for grilled cheese sandwiches.

Skulls don't have noses,
but skulls don't really need noses.

They're more of a cartilage thing.

But most important of all:
skulls are not trying to be scary.

They can't help the way they look.

They just do their job,
and no one says "thank you,"

and some people are even afraid of them.

But not you.
Not you at all.

You love having a safe place
to keep your brain.

You snap your jaws with gusto,
and you love having teeth in your mouth

(until, of course, you lose them).

You love having holes for hearing,

for seeing,

for smelling
and breathing,

and for eating grilled cheese sandwiches.

So tell your friends,
"Nice skull.
It gives your face a good shape."

Tell your family,

"Thanks for helping my skull grow strong and hard."

Take care of your skull,
because you only get one.

And think of how amazing it is
to have such good bones in your body.

 Cool Skull Facts!

Your skull isn't just one single bone—it's made up of twenty-two different smaller bones.

Babies' skulls grow faster than the rest of their bodies. That's why their heads are so big!

When a baby is born, its skull is made up of lots of littler skull bones that fuse together as the baby gets bigger. That's one reason babies need extra attention: to make sure their skulls are growing strong and safe!

The top and back parts of your skull, which houses your brain, is called the "cranium." Your facial bones form the rest of your skull. They include your lower jaws—the part that moves—called the "mandible."

Skull bones aren't totally solid. They have lots of tiny holes in them to let nerves and blood vessels through.

Your head is about 10 percent of your body weight! And your head would be even heavier if your skull didn't have a number of empty spaces in it, like the sinuses between your eyes and nose.

The holes in your skull for your eyes are called "eye sockets," or "orbits," and the hole for your nose is called the "nasal cavity."

Most of your nose is made of cartilage, a thick and rubbery kind of tissue that grows at the ends of bones. But you do have a nasal bone in your skull that holds your nose in place.

Skulls have one of the hardest bones in the whole body: the temporal bone, a section of bone behind and around your ears. It keeps all the little bones inside your ears safe.

The top of your skull is called a "skullcap," which makes sense: it's like a cap at the top of your head!

Other animals have skulls that are much smaller, relative to the sizes of their bodies. But humans have big skulls, because we have big brains to put in them. (This is a good thing.)

Say it again: I love my skull!